The Bursting Balloons Mystery

The Bursting Balloons Mystery

Alexander McCall Smith

illustrations by Ian Bilbey

BLOOMSBURY

Published in Great Britain in 2006 by Bloomsbury Publishing Plc,
36 Soho Square, London, W1D 3QY

First published in the UK by Scholastic Ltd, 1997

A CIP catalogue record of this book is available from the British Library

ISBN 0 7475 8048 0
9780747580485

Printed in Great Britain by Clays Ltd, St Ives Plc

1 3 5 7 9 10 8 6 4 2

All papers used by Bloomsbury Publishing are natural, recyclable products
made from wood grown in well-managed forests. The manufacturing processes
conform to the environmental regulations of the country of origin.

www.mccallsmithbooks.co.uk
www.bloomsbury.com

CHAPTER 1

A Famous Visitor

It had been a hot, hot day, and this meant that Max and Maddy's parents had been very busy. They ran an ice-cream parlour – one of the best in town, with thirty-seven flavours – and ice-cream parlours are always busy when the weather is hot. Max and Maddy had helped them all morning and they were now sitting upstairs getting their breath back.

'That's the busiest we've been for ages,' said Max, wiping his brow. 'It's hard work selling ice cream.'

Maddy looked thoughtful. 'Do you think it's harder than being a private detective?'

Max laughed. 'It's difficult to say. We've only had one case so far.'

Max and Maddy were detectives, just as their parents had been. When their parents' detective agency had been ruined by the tricks of the terrible Professor Claude Sardine, they had started up an ice-cream parlour instead.

But Max and Maddy, who were champion players of Cluedo, had been asked to handle a case themselves – the chocolate money mystery. Now it was over, and they had successfully foiled Professor Sardine's plan to rob the Swiss banks of most of their money. The professor had escaped, and would no doubt be planning a terrible revenge, but for the time being Max and Maddy were very pleased with themselves, and thought that perhaps they would be invited to solve another mystery. But what would it be, and when?

It was while they were thinking about this that Max noticed something peculiar. Just outside the window, floating very slowly upwards, was a large, red balloon. For a moment Max thought he was imagining it, but when he stood up and rubbed his eyes it was still there. Tied to its tail was a length of string, at the end of which fluttered a piece of paper.

By now, Maddy had seen it too, and she quickly opened the window and snatched the string before it disappeared.

'Look,' she said. 'There's a note.'

They unfolded the piece of paper and Max read it out while Maddy tied the bobbing balloon to a chair.

'*To Max and Maddy Twist,*' he read. '*I hope you will not mind this unusual way of catching your attention. People look at balloons, you see, and I find this is the best way of getting a message through. I am downstairs at this very moment, at your front door, having just let go of the balloon. If you look out of the window, you will see me – or rather, you will see my hat, but I shall be beneath the hat. Please let me in. I have something very important to talk about. Signed, Harry Helium, Millionaire.'*

Max folded the note and put it in his pocket. Then he and Maddy went to the window and peered out of it. Sure enough, there below them was a large hat, and underneath it a pair of shoulders and the tips of a pair of shoes.

'Mr Helium?' shouted Max. 'Is that you?'

The hat tilted up and Max and Maddy found themselves looking into a well-known face. They had seen countless pictures of Mr Helium in the newspapers. He was an adventurous sort of man; always engaged in wonderful schemes to break records or raise money for charity.

'It is indeed,' shouted Mr Helium. 'Did you get my message?'

'Yes,' said Max. 'Thank you very much. We'll come right down and let you in.'

Mr Helium walked into the room and placed his hat carefully on a chair. He was a tall man, with a beard, and a glint in his eye that made him look rather like a pirate. But unlike pirates, who almost always scowl, Mr Helium smiled broadly as he spoke. Max and Maddy could tell at once that he was a kind man, whose aim in life was probably to give fun to people. They both liked him immediately. Here was a person who spread a lot of happiness.

'You may have heard of me,' said Mr Helium. 'But do you know how I made my fortune?'

Max and Maddy shook their heads. Rich people often made their fortune in a very dull way, but something told them that Mr Helium was different.

'I made things out of rubber,' said Mr Helium, smiling broadly. 'Tennis shoes with special rubber soles that made it possible to jump high enough to hit any ball. Inflatable rubber ducks to teach babies to swim and inflatable rubber babies to teach ducks to swim. Rubber mugs that would bounce back on to the table if you dropped them. And balloons, of course. Just about every party balloon you've ever blown up will have been made by one of my factories.'

Mr Helium paused. 'Then, after I had made my fortune, I decided to have some fun, and I took up travelling around in balloons. I crossed the North Pole in one go – I was the first person to do that – and I also floated from China to Africa in the space of five weeks, never touching the ground once.'

Max and Maddy were fascinated. They had read about Mr Helium's exploits in the newspapers, but now they were hearing it from the man himself. It was very exciting.

'Have you ever been in a balloon?' asked Mr Helium. 'Do you know what it's like?'

'No,' said Maddy. 'We've been in an aeroplane, in a train, in a cable car and a bus as well. But we've never gone anywhere by balloon.'

Mr Helium nodded. 'Well, it's a most wonderful experience. It's so quiet, you see. All you hear is the sound of the wind and there's not much between you and the ground down below – just a little basket. It's like one of those dreams we have when we can fly. Do you ever have them?'

'Yes,' said Max. 'I often dream that I can fly. It's wonderful. And then I wake up and feel terribly disappointed when I realise I can't.'

Mr Helium smiled. 'I like to make dreams come true,' he said. 'That's what I like to do.'

There was silence for a moment. It seemed as if Mr Helium was thinking about something. When he spoke again, his smile had disappeared.

'As you may know,' he said, 'I live in New York. I've been planning a race – a balloon race – from New York, all the way over America and up into Canada. The race would finish in Vancouver, which is right on the other side, at the edge of the ocean.'

'That's a long way,' said Maddy. She was

good at maps, and she could imagine just what lay between New York and Vancouver. There were wide prairies, the Great Lakes, and, of course, the balloons would have to go over the famous Rocky Mountains. It would not be easy.

'Yes,' said Mr Helium. 'It will not be easy. But for the person who wins, it will certainly have been worthwhile. The prize, you see, is very special. It's a gold balloon, mounted on a gold base, and worth one million and one dollars!'

'That's a wonderful prize!' exclaimed Max. 'Surely everybody would want to win that?'

'That's true,' said Mr Helium. 'But only the best balloonists will be allowed to enter. We don't want people who know nothing about ballooning getting stuck in telephone wires or coming down in the middle of the Great Lakes.'

'What happens if you fly into telephone wires or a very tall tree?' asked Maddy. 'How do you get down?'

Mr Helium frowned. 'With great difficulty,' he said. 'If you've got a rope, you try to let yourself down. If you haven't got a rope, well, you just hope that somebody comes along to rescue you. I know people who have stayed up there for days before people came to get them down. A friend of mine spent four weeks – yes, *four* weeks – in his basket on the top of a tree before his rescuers

arrived. Fortunately he had enough sandwiches and water to see him through. And the squirrels helped him too, I believe. They brought him nuts.'

Max wondered what it would be like to spend four weeks up a tree. He did not think that he would like to try it.

Mr Helium continued to explain his race. 'Everybody is very excited about the race,' he said. 'All the best balloonists from all over the world came to enter for it. They came from Paris and Rome and Cairo and Singapore. And we even had somebody from Timbuktu. They all wanted to enter, but I'm only taking the six best.'

The famous millionaire now lowered his voice. 'Which makes it all the worse that something's gone badly wrong.'

'What is it?' asked Max.

Mr Helium's expression was grave. 'Somebody is planning to ruin the race. Even before it has started, people are finding things going wrong with their practice flights. Baskets have had lead strapped on to them from below to make it more difficult to take off. Gas has been let out of cylinders to make the burners go out. Somebody even had his matches stolen, so he couldn't start his burner when the air in his balloon went cold! It's been one thing after another.'

'But how can we help you?' asked Max after a moment. 'We aren't really balloonists.'

Mr Helium brushed this aside. 'It's not balloonists I'm looking for,' he said quickly. 'I want a couple of detectives to come with me to New York and find out what's happening. And I need them immediately. The race is due to start tomorrow.'

Max opened his mouth to talk. He was about to say that with all this hot weather they were rather busy helping in the ice-cream parlour and it would be difficult to get away. He did not have time to speak, however, as Mr Helium had dropped to his knees and was beseeching Max and Maddy to agree.

'You can't let me down,' he said. 'The race is for charity. All the money it raises will be going to the Home for Children Whose Parents Have Disappeared in Balloons. You can't let the children down, can you?'

Max and Maddy looked at one another. Of course they couldn't.

'We'll help,' said Maddy. 'What do we have to do?'

'Come with me to New York,' said Mr Helium. 'The plane leaves in . . .' He looked at his large watch, with its numerous dials and buttons. 'In exactly forty-five minutes. If we hurry, we'll just catch it!'

Max and Maddy quickly asked their parents who, having been private detectives themselves, knew just how important this trip would be. So they said, without a moment's hesitation, 'Of course you can go. Have a good time!'

CHAPTER 2

New York

Mr Helium lived in an extremely tall building in New York. When Max and Maddy saw it for the first time, they were not sure how many floors there were, but they were sure that it was no less than eighty. Nor did they guess from the outside just how luxurious it would be once you crossed into the entrance hall with its uniformed attendant. The floors in the hall were all made of marble, the ceilings were painted with scenes of clouds and angels, and all the buttons in the elevator looked as if they were pure gold.

Mr Helium, of course, lived right up at the top, in the penthouse. From his sitting room, which had one wall made entirely of glass, you could look out over the other skyscrapers and down to the streets so very far below. It was breathtaking, and it made Max, who was a little bit afraid of heights, the tiniest bit dizzy.

Mr Helium pointed out the sights to the two children, while one of the maids served them with glasses of chilled fruit juice and chocolate biscuits.

'That's the Empire State Building over there,' said Mr Helium, pointing to the famous structure that the children had seen in so many pictures. 'And that, over there, in the distance, is the Statue of Liberty.'

The children were thrilled. They had

always wanted to go to New York, and now here they were, looking out over all these famous sights. And who better to see New York with than Mr Helium?

Of course, they were all rather tired from the flight, and they decided that the best thing to do would be to go off and sleep. There would be plenty of time for sightseeing later on. Or so they thought! When they awoke, many hours later, it was late morning. Mr Helium was already up and waiting to welcome them in the breakfast room. Max and Maddy could tell immediately that something was wrong. The normally cheerful millionaire was sitting with his head in his hands. He looked up when the children came in and let out a deep sigh.

'More bad news,' he said miserably. 'Read this.'

He handed Maddy a telegram, which she unfolded and read out to her brother.

'Regret to say that I must pull out of the race,' the telegram began. *'Somebody cut*

the ropes of my balloon yesterday when it was tied up in my garden. The balloon floated away and we just can't find it. Very sorry.'

'That comes from one of America's best balloonists,' explained Mr Helium. 'And that balloon of his was one of the finest in the country.'

Max shook his head. 'Why would somebody want to do such a thing?' he asked.

Mr Helium shrugged his shoulders. 'I suppose somebody wants to stop other people winning,' he said. 'They want to win

the golden balloon themselves. And they seem prepared to go to any lengths to do so.'

'We must stop them,' said Max decisively. 'We must enter the race ourselves and make sure that nobody cheats.' (This was actually a rather brave suggestion, considering Max's fear of heights.)

'But I can't enter the race myself,' said Mr Helium. 'I'm the person who's organising the whole thing. It wouldn't be fair if I won.'

Max thought for a moment. 'If you won,' he said, 'you could give the golden balloon to the person who came second. Think how pleased they would be!'

The millionaire looked thoughtful. 'You know, that's an excellent idea! We'll enter ourselves.'

'I can't wait,' said Maddy. 'When can we start?'

'Right now,' said Mr Helium, rising to his feet. 'I shall call my driver, and he'll take us out to the balloon shed straight away. We'll have plenty of time to get everything ready.'

CHAPTER 3

The Race Begins

Everybody was very excited. The president of the United States himself had agreed to start the race and was going to fire the starting pistol for the six balloons which were going to take part. And the president's wife, the first lady, who had heard that Max and Maddy were going to be helping Mr Helium, had brought them a large fruit cake which she had baked for them herself in the White House kitchens.

'You might get hungry on the journey,' she said to them. 'So here is a cake for you and Mr Helium to nibble on.'

Mr Helium was nervous that something terrible could still happen to stop the race getting under way, and so he was delighted when at last all six balloons were lined up, hovering just a few metres above the ground, waiting for the start.

It was a very exciting line-up, with only the best balloonists present. They came from every corner of the globe. There, sitting in their red, white and blue basket were the twin French balloonists, Jacques and Henri Montgolfier, descendants of a long line of brave French balloonists. From Italy there was Count Alberto Ozono, an elegant-looking man with a long, twirly moustache and very fancy ballooning trousers. Next to him, from the other side of the world, was the famous Australian balloonist, Bonzer Williams. He had crossed the great Australian desert by balloon not once, but twice, in both directions, and had even landed on top of Ayers Rock. He'd also had many other narrow escapes, including landing in the Tasman Sea and having to keep the sharks away with a single boomerang which he happened to have with him.

Honoria Honeyman was there too, suspended in her basket beneath a great yellow balloon, almost twice as big as any of the others. She and her co-pilot, Dolores Dogwood, were from Texas, and had completed numerous heroic balloon trips, including one over the Arctic in a fur-lined balloon! They were very courageous indeed.

And finally, next to them, was Mr Peter Zambuck from Zambia, the bravest balloonist in Africa. He was well known for his famous flight over Mount Kilimanjaro when he had fallen out of the basket and had been saved by having his ankle caught in a rope. The balloon had eventually come to earth safely, bringing Mr Zambuck dangling below it, and he had slid down the neck of an inquisitive giraffe who had stretched up its head to see what was happening.

There they all were – lined up, waiting for the president to start the race.

The president of the United States stood on a platform just in front of the balloons and made a speech. He spoke for rather a long time, and most of the speech was about himself and his plans (which had nothing to do with balloons), but everybody was very polite and listened as best they could. He went on so long, though, that a couple of the balloons had to light their burners again, just to keep above the ground.

Then at last he finished and, while the crowd stood breathless with excitement, he picked up the starting pistol and fired it into the air.

BANG! The pistol shot rang out and the

crowd gave
a cheer. But
then, oh no! A
terrible, terrible
thing happened.
Somebody had
sabotaged the very
pistol with which
the president began
the race. Instead of
firing a blank, which
such pistols normal-
ly do, this one fired a
real bullet. And this
bullet shot out of
the barrel and
went straight
through the
middle of Mr
Zambuck's
balloon! With
a loud pop,
the balloon let

out all its air and sank to the ground, giving Mr Zambuck a nasty jolt.

It was a terrible start, but Mr Helium made up his mind in seconds. The race would go ahead, even if there were only five balloons left. It was terribly bad luck for Mr Zambuck, and it was also very embarrassing for the president. He turned quite red, in fact, and everybody looked at him as if he were to blame. The first lady was particularly cross.

'Look what you've done,' she scolded, wagging a finger at him. 'Here you are, president of the United States, and you can't even fire a starting pistol without causing damage. I give up! I just give up! Where you would be without me to help you, I have no idea!'

Max and Maddy knew, however, that it was not his fault at all. Somebody had sabotaged the beginning of the race. But who was he, and what would he do next? And could they stop him before he did it?

They soon settled down to the race. It would take many days to cross America, and they had quite a lot to do. Maddy was in charge of navigation and had to sort out the maps, and Mr Helium operated the burners. Max was in charge of sandbags and, once he'd got used to being at such a height (and could open his eyes), keeping a lookout for obstructions.

Of course, you are at the mercy of the winds when you're in a balloon. If they blow in one direction, then you go that way until they decide to change their minds and blow in another. All that you can do, if you're going in the wrong direction, is to land. Then, when the winds go the right way, off you can go again.

That first day, the wind was blowing quite hard from the east, and the balloons all set off at a fine speed. The children had a grand view from the basket of Mr Helium's balloon, and Max's fear soon turned to excitement. All around them, stretching for miles in every direction, were the round shapes of the other balloons. And down below them, like a great patchwork carpet, were the fields and farms and roads.

At lunchtime they picnicked in the basket, suspended several thousand feet above the ground. Then, later that afternoon, when they were drifting along in the breeze, watching the fields unfold beneath them,

Max noticed something odd. There was a bird, quite a large one, circling up above them. Could it be an eagle? It certainly looked large enough.

Max tugged at Mr Helium's sleeve and pointed up.

'Do you get eagles this close to New York?' he asked.

Mr Helium shaded his eyes with his hand and stared up at the sky.

'Eagles?' he said. 'Up in the mountains, perhaps, but not . . .'

He stopped. The bird had dropped a little bit lower and they could now see what it was. It was no bird; it was a plane, a model plane, with a whining engine that could now be heard above the gentle sound of the wind in the ropes.

'What's that doing up there?' asked Max.

Mr Helium looked puzzled. 'Somebody must be controlling it from down below,' he said. 'But why would they fly it this high?'

As he spoke, the plane dropped a little bit

lower and now began to circle directly above the balloon.

'It's getting too close,' shouted Mr Helium. 'If it gets any closer it could fly into the balloon and tear it.'

'What can we do?' asked Maddy. 'Do you think whoever it is down there has seen what's happening?'

Mr Helium looked grim. 'I think they have,' he said. 'And I think that's exactly what they want. They want to force us down!'

The little buzzing plane was now getting closer and closer, and Mr Helium had no choice but to open a vent in the balloon and let some of the hot air escape. As the air hissed out, they felt the balloon drop sharply. It was rather like the feeling you get on a roller-coaster when you plummet downhill and leave your stomach behind.

For a few moments, they thought they were safe, but no sooner had they lost height than the plane swooped down again and started buzzing around immediately above them. Again Mr Helium had to open the vent and let the balloon sink.

Suddenly Maddy gave a cry. They had been so busy dealing with the threat from the model plane, they hadn't noticed how low they were . . . and that they were drifting straight towards a towering tree!

'Quick,' she shouted. 'Up!'

Mr Helium turned on the burner and a great flame shot out, rather like dragon's breath. This made the balloon lift over the top of the tree, just. But as they did so, the angry little plane gave a swoop and with a terrible tearing noise ripped a hole in the balloon before it shot up and flew into the clouds.

They were lucky that they were so close to the ground when this happened. The balloon went down, but because it was so low they felt no more than a gentle bump when they landed.

'He's brought us down,' cried Mr Helium in bitter disappointment. 'We're out of the race now! It's all over for us.'

Max, however, was not so sure. He had climbed out of the balloon and was examining the tear in the cloth. He never travelled without a needle and thread to sew on any buttons which might pop off, and now this would come in useful.

'I can fix it,' he said to Mr Helium. 'We'll camp here for the night and set off again first thing tomorrow. We should catch up with the others if we leave early enough.'

As it happened, they had come down in a splendid place to camp, and they spent that night under the stars, each wrapped in a warm sleeping-bag, looking up into the great night sky. Maddy went to sleep wondering what tomorrow would bring. Mr Helium went to sleep wondering whether everything was all right with the other balloonists. And Max dozed off thinking, *I wonder who's trying to sabotage the race? Could it be one of the other balloonists?* The next morning dawned bright and clear. As Max opened his eyes, he quickly cast a glance towards the balloon. Fortunately it was still there, and nobody seemed to have interfered with it.

Max cooked everybody a large breakfast on the camp stove from the basket, and then, when they had brushed their teeth in a nearby river, the great balloon was inflated again and off they set. Because they left so early, and because the wind was strong, they soon caught up with the others and saw them taking off from their own campsites. There was the wonderful yellow balloon of Honoria Honeyman and Dolores Dogwood, who had spent the night on top of a small hill. There was the pure white balloon of Count Alberto Ozono, who had come down in the middle of a parking lot. And there were the other two, the balloons belonging to the Montgolfier twins and Bonzer Williams, both in good order.

The three drifted on, riding the wind, and soon were high enough to have a good view of the countryside. This had changed a little, and there were more woods, which Max was busy inspecting from above when it happened.

There was really no warning. Honoria Honeyman and her friend, Dolores, were also enjoying the view when the bottom of their basket fell out. It gave way with a sudden tearing sound and dropped completely away, fluttering down to the ground below.

It could have been an awful tragedy. Fortunately Honoria was sitting on the edge of the basket when it happened. Dolores, however, fell right out of the bottom and tumbled head over heels towards the tree-tops. At the sight of this, Honoria acted with lightning speed. Pulling at the rope which operated the air vent, she allowed half of the hot air in the balloon to gush out. This made the balloon fall like a stone, quite as fast as Dolores was falling, if not even a bit faster.

Poor Dolores thought that nothing would save her, and was astonished when the basket shot past her on the way to the ground.

'Grab hold of this rope,' shouted Honoria to her friend.

Dolores snatched at the rope as she tumbled down. Then, when she saw that her friend had seized it, Honoria rapidly untied as many sandbags as she could reach. This

suddenly made the balloon much lighter, and, almost without delay, the basket began to lift, dragging poor Dolores up beneath it.

It was just in time: Dolores' feet were almost touching the trees when she began to rise. Seeing that her friend was safe, Honoria breathed a sigh of relief and gently landed the balloon in a nearby clearing.

'That's it!' said Dolores, letting go of the rope. 'I've had enough of this ballooning business! I'm walking home from here.'

'That's exactly what I feel too,' agreed Honoria. 'I've had enough as well.'

Max and Maddy watched all this from above. They had no doubt that the bottom of the basket had been interfered with by somebody. The saboteur had struck again, and almost caused terrible injury. Somehow they had to stop him before another balloon was brought down. But they still had no clues and now there were only four balloons left. And it was the second day of the race.

CHAPTER 4

The Saboteur Is Exposed

Max thought hard about what had happened.

'Something's puzzling me,' he said to Maddy, as they drifted away from the trees in which Honoria and Dolores had so nearly been wrecked. 'How is it that the cheat is still managing to sabotage the race when we are far away from the start line? How does he know where we are?'

Maddy scratched her head. 'He must be following us,' she said.

'But how could he do that?' said Max. 'We've been going over all sorts of rough country. Most of the time there are no roads below.'

Maddy was thoughtful. 'Do you mean . . . ?' She broke off. Surely Max couldn't mean that.

'Yes,' said Max. 'That's exactly what I mean. I am sure that the cheat is in one of the balloons. That's how he knows where we are. That's how he was able to sabotage Honoria's basket.'

Mr Helium, who had overheard all this, gave a shudder. He was looking at the other balloons, which were drifting peacefully over a thin layer of cloud. The thought that in one of them was a ruthless cheat was not a comfortable one.

'How can we find out who it is?' he asked

Max. 'They all look quite innocent. Look at them!'

They looked down at the other balloons, which were drifting along a bit below them. The Montgolfier twins were in the lead now, closely followed by Count Ozono. Mr Helium and the children were in third place, and finally, a little behind, was Bonzer Williams.

Max suddenly smiled. 'I've had an idea,' he said. 'Could we get within shouting distance of each of them?'

'I suppose so,' said Mr Helium. 'If we drop down a bit we might get close enough to the Montgolfiers and the count. Then we could drop back a bit and approach Bonzer Williams.'

'Please do that,' said Max. 'I think I might be able to find out who's who.'

Mr Helium made the balloon descend and they were soon close enough to the Montgolfiers to shout across the empty bit of sky that separated them. Max leaned out of the edge of the basket and cupped his hands round his mouth.

'*Bonjour!*' he shouted. '*Ça va?* (This was French, of course, and meant: 'Hallo! How are things going?')

The Montgolfiers looked up.

'*Bien,*' they shouted in perfect harmony.

'*Très bien!*' (And this meant: 'All's going well – very well!')

Max turned to Mr Helium. 'Now could we go a little bit lower please?'

Mr Helium looked puzzled. This was all very strange, but Max seemed to know what he was doing. The balloon dropped slightly and now they were getting closer to Count Ozono.

'Count Ozono!' shouted Max. 'You're looking rather *porco* today!'

Count Ozono glanced up. Even from some distance away, they could tell he was smiling, as the sunlight flashed off his brilliant white teeth.

'Why, thank you!' he said. 'Thank you very much.'

'Aha!' said Max to Mr Helium. 'Now just one left. Let's see what Bonzer Williams has to say.'

They soon came within shouting distance of Bonzer Williams' balloon and Max leaned out again to hail the famous Australian.

'How are you doing mate?' he called out.

Bonzer Williams waved cheerfully. 'Fair dinkum, cobber,' he shouted. 'No worries!'

'Good,' shouted Max and sat back in the basket. He looked gravely at Mr Helium and made his announcement.

'We now know exactly who the cheat is,' he said. 'Count Ozono is not an Italian at all! He's an imposter!'

Maddy gasped in astonishment. 'But how do you know that?' she asked.

'I called him a pig, in Italian,' answered Max. 'It was a terrible insult. And he said thank you. That goes to show that he's not an Italian at all. There may be a real Count Ozono, but that man in the balloon over there is not him. He can't even speak Italian. He's somebody else altogether!'

After this amazing discovery, they made very good progress. By the time it started to get dark, the balloons had covered hundreds of miles. It seemed to Max that they now must be right in the very middle of America, and Maddy confirmed this when she showed them the map.

The balloons all came down that evening at the edge of a large lake. Although they were not too close to one another, Max could see exactly where the others had landed, and when the sun eventually went down, he could see the dots of light from the camp fires which the balloonists had made.

After supper, as they sat around their fire, Max explained his plan. 'I think that we should go off and take a look at Count Ozono,' he said. 'If we're quiet enough, he won't see us.'

Mr Helium looked doubtful. 'It could be dangerous,' he said. 'What if he spots us?'

'He won't,' said Max. 'We shall be as quiet as mice, and it's a pitch dark night. There's not even a moon.'

Maddy shivered. This was another of her brother's plans, and she knew that they could be scary. But she also knew that once he made up his mind about something, then it would be very difficult to get him to change it.

So they agreed to set off, creeping through the undergrowth, until they found Count Ozono's campsite. There he was, sitting beside a fire, finishing off the dinner he had prepared for himself. And as they watched this scene from the shelter of the surrounding trees, they saw a remarkable thing.

Count Ozono stood up and stretched. Then, in full view of the three hidden watchers, he peeled off his false eyebrows, removed his artificial moustache, and wiped the make-up from his brow.

Max and Maddy drew in their breath.

'Professor Sardine!' they hissed together. 'It's him!'

They crawled away as quietly as they could and then broke into a run that took them all the way back to their own camp. There, panting and breathless, they sat down to explain to Mr Helium just who Professor Sardine was.

'He's the most ruthless villain,' said Max. 'We should have realised it was him well before this. He ruined our parents' detective agency, you see.'

'And he almost succeeded in robbing the Swiss banks of all their money,' added Maddy. 'Until we stopped him, that is.'

Mr Helium listened gravely as Max and Maddy finished their account of Professor

Sardine's evil doings. 'We shall wait until tomorrow morning,' he said. 'Then, immediately after breakfast, we shall take off and announce to all the other contestants that Count Ozono is a dangerous saboteur. Then, as soon as we reach a town or village, we shall descend and tell the police all about it.'

It seemed like a perfectly reasonable thing to do, and on that note Max and Maddy slid into their sleeping bags while Mr Helium put out the fire. They were glad that they had found Professor Sardine, but the thought that he was only a short distance away filled them all with anxiety. Could *you* sleep if you knew that one of the most dangerous men in the world was just on the other side of a wood? I don't think I could, but then Max and Maddy, and their famous friend Mr Helium, were all a good bit braver than I am. They slept quite well, and by the time morning came they were ready to stand up to the evil Professor Sardine and all his nasty tricks.

CHAPTER 5

Up into the Ozone Layer

They woke early the next morning and had soon prepared the balloon for take-off. Mr Helium started the burner while Max and Maddy held the mouth of the balloon open, and with a lovely crumpling sound the great bag filled with hot air. Then, having loaded all their camping things into the basket, they cast off from the ground.

The other balloons were almost ready to take off, but Mr Helium's balloon was up first. As they rose above the trees, though, they saw that Professor Sardine's balloon was beginning to rise too. He was downwind of them, and so they floated slowly towards him.

They were soon within shouting distance of the white balloon and they saw its evil occupant, back in his disguise, sitting in the basket, watching them suspiciously.

'Count Ozono?' called Mr Helium suddenly.

'Yes?' came the reply from the other basket.

'Or should I say . . . *Professor Sardine!*' cried out Mr Helium. 'Oh yes, that's who you are! And you thought that you would get the golden balloon by cheating! Well, we know who you are now, and the game is most definitely up.'

Professor Sardine stared at Mr Helium, his eyes filled with rage.

'You fool!' he shouted. 'You ignorant gas-bag! I'll show you what happens to those who meddle with Professor Claude Sardine! I'll fix you – and that includes those two nasty little brats with you. I'll fix them too, good and proper this time!'

The other balloonists, when they heard this, turned and stared at the white balloon and its occupant. Professor Sardine seemed to be busy with something, and suddenly everybody saw what it was. He was releasing ballast, every last bit of it, and like a cork popping out of a bottle, his balloon shot up in the air. Once it was a bit higher, the winds caught it, and it sped away into the clouds, leaving everybody else far down below.

The other balloonists all shouted their congratulations to Mr Helium and the children.

'We've seen the last of him!' shouted the Montgolfier twins. 'Good riddance too!'

Max and Maddy were more cautious. They

knew Professor Sardine of old, and they knew that it was not so easy to get rid of him. They suspected the worst – they suspected that he had a plan that he was putting into operation. There was some further nastiness afoot and it could happen at any time.

It happened, in fact, only five minutes later. As the balloons reached the right height, everybody turned off their burners and sat back in their baskets. Everybody, that is, except for the Montgolfier twins. From their basket came the sound of shouts and cries as they struggled with the valves of their burner. Somebody had interfered with them, and it was impossible to shut down the flames. So, instead of floating peacefully along, their balloon continued to rise.

'They're in deep trouble,' said Mr Helium, when he saw what was happening. 'Their balloon's just going to go further up and up until they hit the ozone layer. Then they won't be able to breathe.'

Max and Maddy were horrified. So this was Professor Sardine's plan; and what a terrible thing it was.

'But we have to help them,' Max cried. 'We must go up after them.'

Mr Helium nodded desperately. 'Yes,' he said. 'We'll have to do something!'

At this, they turned on their own burner again and released some sandbags to make the balloon lighter. This made them rise quickly, and soon they were catching up with the Montgolfier twins, whose burner was still belching flames and sending them further up. The air was getting colder now, and Max noticed that it was getting harder to breathe. The ozone layer could not be far off!

'Throw us a rope,' shouted Mr Helium to the Montgolfiers.

The Frenchmen looked down and began to struggle with a coil of rope on the side of

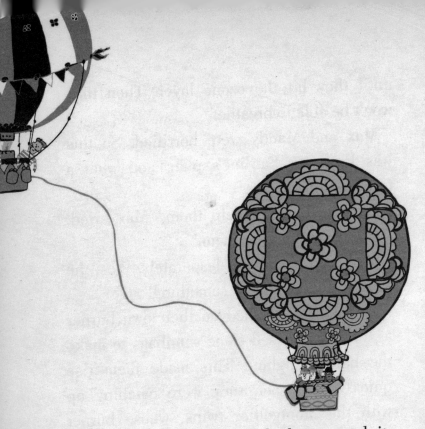

their basket. When they had unwound it, they threw one end down. Maddy reached out as it swung past her side of the basket and, on Mr Helium's instructions, tied it to the basket.

'Good,' said Mr Helium. 'Now, Max, pull on that cord and release most of our air.'

'But . . .' protested Max. 'But if I do that then . . .'

'Just do as I say,' shouted Mr Helium. 'And quickly! We haven't a moment to lose.'

Max realised that Mr Helium was the captain and that he should obey. And so, although the earth was terribly far below, and although it seemed a very long way to fall, he did as he was told.

The effect was immediate. As Mr Helium's balloon lost its air, it grew heavy and began to sink. This dragged the Montgolfier balloon down after them, and within a few minutes, they both drifted slowly down to land in a field, with no more than a tiny bump.

Mr Helium helped the Montgolfier twins to repair their burner and then, when everything was ready, they both took off again. It had been a narrow escape, but with any luck now everything would go smoothly – for the time being at least!

CHAPTER 6

Things Go Wrong Again

It took a little time for them to catch up with Bonzer Williams, and for a moment it even looked as if they might overtake the Australian balloon. But they had overlooked one thing. Professor Sardine had promised to get even with them, and now, as they floated up towards the clouds, they discovered that this was exactly what he had done.

The gas cylinder attached to the burner was nearly empty, so Mr Helium set about changing it. It was then that he discovered the spare was empty. It had a tiny hole in it, so tiny that no one had noticed the gas slowly leaking out. But it had all escaped.

'Professor Sardine must have sneaked over last night while we were asleep,' said Maddy grimly, 'and punctured it.'

This was a disaster. They were now flying over the Rocky Mountains, with their great peaks and tree-filled valleys, and the air in the balloon was getting colder and colder. This meant that they would sink slowly towards the ground until they landed in the middle of the trees or, worse still, on a slippery glacier.

They tried to catch the attention of Bonzer Williams and the Montgolfiers, who were some way off but who could still just be seen. They waved their hands and shouted, but the wind swallowed their words. Max even took off his T-shirt and waved that, but it was all to no avail. They were just too far away.

There was only one thing for them to do, and that was to go down now. That way, at least they could use the last of the hot air in the balloon to choose a safe spot to land.

Max and Maddy kept a lookout over the edge of the basket while Mr Helium opened the vent. They were searching for a clearing, but all they saw in the valley below them were tall trees and a swift, icy river.

'We're going to land on top of a tree,' wailed Maddy. 'We'll be stuck there for ever!'

Max shook his head. 'There's bound to be a clearing,' he said. 'Somewhere.'

But all that they saw was a spiky canopy of green treetops, until quite miraculously the trees gave out to an area of grass and bushes.

'There,' shouted Max excitedly. 'Just keep us up for a little while longer.'

The tired balloon limped along for a few

metres more, and just cleared the last of the trees before it sank down on to the grassy floor of the clearing.

'We've done it!' shouted Maddy. 'We're safe!'

Max was silent. He was not so sure about how safe they were. It was all very well landing in one piece, but where had they landed? Right in the middle of the most remote valley of the Rocky Mountains. Nobody had seen them come down, and they were miles and miles from the nearest help. It was as bad as being shipwrecked, or almost as bad.

Mr Helium was also rather worried.

'I don't know what to do,' he said, after a while. 'We could stay here, I suppose, and hope that somebody comes to rescue us, but I'm not sure if they'd find us.'

Max said nothing. He was thinking very hard. The best way of getting out of a remote spot like this was by air. And they had a balloon, after all, even if the balloon had collapsed in a crumpled heap around them. What they needed was some hot air to fill it up again, but they had no gas left to burn . . .

What else would burn? Max suddenly smiled.

'I've got an idea,' he said. 'A really good one.'

Maddy groaned. Her brother's ideas were usually terribly dangerous, and sometimes she wished that he wouldn't keep having them.

'We're out here in the middle of the mountains,' began Max.

'That's true,' said Mr Helium sadly.

'Surrounded by trees,' went on Max.

'That's also true,' Mr Helium said.

'And trees are made of wood,' said Max, smiling. 'And wood, you remember, burns rather well.'

Maddy now began to smile too. 'We could use wood instead of the gas burner!' she exclaimed. 'Why, Max, your ideas are always so good!'

Mr Helium was smiling too now. 'What a splendid idea,' he said. 'Let's start collecting wood right away.'

The three stranded balloonists all went off in separate directions, scouring the edge of the forest for suitable pieces of dry wood. Mr Helium found several dead branches and was soon busy breaking these up. Maddy found some extremely useful twigs which they could use for kindling, and Max, being a little bit more adventurous than the other two, wandered off a short distance right into the wood.

It was to prove a terrible mistake. As he walked beneath the trees, he thought he heard a noise. He stopped, and listened carefully. There are often all sorts of sounds in a forest, and what you think might be an animal may turn out to be little more than a crackling underfoot. But this did *sound* like a grunt . . .

Max decided to make his way back to the balloon. It would be best to be on the safe side.

Back at the basket, Mr Helium had placed the tin from the first lady's cake on top of the burner under the mouth of the balloon and had piled twigs and small branches in it. Spare wood had been neatly stacked in the bottom of the basket. It would probably be rather uncomfortable, but at least they would get back in the air.

Max and Maddy held the mouth of the balloon open while Mr Helium lit the fire. It took a little time, and there was a great deal of smoke, but at last the balloon began to fill with hot air and inflate.

'It's going to work!' shouted Mr Helium. 'Hop into the basket now.'

The two children climbed back into the basket and blew as hard as they could on the fire. They could see that it was going to be some time before the balloon was warm enough to take off. But it was definitely going to work!

Then they heard the grunts. Max spun round and looked towards the edge of the forest. 'Oh, no!' he shouted. 'Look over there!' So that was what he had disturbed! A grizzly bear, the fiercest and most dangerous creature in the Rockies!

Maddy and Mr Helium gasped as they saw what was coming. The bear, which was extremely large, was ambling over in their direction, very angry at being disturbed. His mouth, which was open in an unfriendly snarl, showed a row of gleaming white fangs, and his claws, which he had extended in his annoyance, were like ivory knives.

Max looked up at the balloon. It was clearly almost ready to take off, but not quite, and the bear was getting closer and closer and snarling more and more angrily.

'We'll never make it,' groaned Maddy. 'The bear will be here in no time.'

Then she suddenly spotted the first lady's cake, which Mr Helium had tipped out of its tin. They had been looking forward to eating it, but this was an emergency, and in an emergency you have to make sacrifices. She began to rip off its paper wrapping.

'This is a fine time to eat cake,' said Max angrily. 'We're in the middle of a bear attack, and all you can think about is your stomach!'

But Maddy paid no attention to him. She lifted up the cake and, using all her strength, threw it in the direction of the approaching grizzly.

At first the bear thought that Maddy had thrown a rock at him and he gave a loud snarl. But then, with his bear's sensitive nose, he realised that this was a most unusual rock. He stopped, and bent down to sniff at the cake on the ground. *Mmm! Lovely smell, this! And what about a taste? Ooh!*

The grizzly bear was too busy eating the large presidential cake to notice that he was giving his enemies time to escape. So while he surrounded himself with crumbs, they fanned the fire for all they were worth until, with a slight rocking motion, the basket began to rise into the air.

'We've made it!' shouted Max. 'We're on our way.'

It was rather unwise of him to shout out like this, as the bear, attracted by his voice, ran over to try and reach them before they escaped. His slashing claws just about touched the bottom of the basket, but did not quite make it.

From the safety of their balloon, the three balloonists all gave a huge sigh of relief and watched as the bear grew smaller and smaller below them. It had been a very narrow escape and they hoped that whatever happened next would not be quite as frightening as that.

CHAPTER 7

Sorting Out Professor Sardine

Of course they were now far behind the remaining two balloons. This did not matter, as Mr Helium did not particularly want to win his own race, but he was keen to catch up and make sure Professor Sardine didn't try any more evil tricks.

The firewood fire worked well, and carried

them safely over the Rockies. Then, with the last mountainside behind them, they saw a little town down below and decided to land for the night. They would be able to buy more gas there, and stock up with provisions. They might even buy a cake, Mr Helium said, to make up for the disappointment of having fed the first lady's cake to the unfriendly grizzly.

They landed gently in a farmer's field and the farmer came out to meet them. He was very friendly, and most interested in the balloon.

'It's a funny thing to have two balloons in one day,' he said. 'Usually we get none in a whole year. Now two in one day!'

Max pricked up his ears.

'Two?' he said. 'Where's the other?'

'A big white balloon landed over there in my brother's field,' said the farmer, pointing towards a farm in the distance. 'It arrived a couple of hours ago.'

This news put an anxious frown on Max's

face. That could only be one person: Professor Sardine, in cunning disguise as Count Alberto Ozono!

The farmer was very kind. He and his wife prepared them a delicious meal of sweet-corn, roast potatoes and apple pie – all from the farm – and then showed them to the rooms where they were to spend the night. They all said goodnight to one another and went off to bed – all, that is, except for Max. He closed his door behind him, but he did not go to bed. Rather, he waited until every-body else would be sound asleep and then, on tiptoes so as to make no sound, he crept out of the house and into the darkness.

Max had another plan. This time he had not told anybody about it, because he was sure that they would say that it would not work. It was possible too, that Mr Helium, fun though he was, might feel that it was just a little bit too dangerous and forbid him to do it. So Max decided to act on his own.

Max made his way stealthily through the dark night. He tried to feel brave, but it was quite hard, and every so often he stopped for a little shiver, half of cold and half of fear. At one point he had a terrible fright, and almost ran all the way back to the farmhouse. This was when he bumped into a scarecrow, who looked just like . . . Well, just like Professor Sardine, he thought!

Then he carried out his plan. It took a lot of bravery, and quite a bit of luck. But everything went very well and within an hour he was back in the safety of the farmhouse. *What was the plan?* you ask. Wait. All will be revealed shortly.

The next morning the three set off as the sun came up over the Rockies. The farmer and his wife helped them to inflate the balloon, and gave shouts of joy and excitement as it rose above their fields.

'Come back soon!' cried the farmer. 'You'll always be welcome!'

'We shall!' shouted Mr Helium. 'And thank you for all your kindness!'

The farmer shouted something else, and pointed, but they were now too high and did not hear what he said. What he had seen, in fact, was Professor Sardine's own balloon rising above its distant field. The wicked professor was setting out too, and no doubt planning a further bout of mischief.

It was not long before they saw Professor Sardine. Because the wind was carrying them both in the same direction, they drifted closer and closer together, and this made Mr Helium a little bit worried. Max, however, had his plan, and he realised that now was the time to put it into operation.

'Let's try to go as high as we can,' he said to Mr Helium. 'Then we might be able to get away from Professor Sardine and reach the others in time to warn them that he's on his way.'

Mr Helium agreed that this was a good idea and he switched on the burner to give them more hot air. Straight away the balloon responded, rising swiftly into the clear morning sky.

When Professor Sardine saw this, he immediately gave chase, turning on his own burner. This was exactly what Max wanted him to do.

'So far so good,' muttered Max.

'What was that?' asked Mr Helium. 'Did you say something?'

'Nothing important,' said Max. 'But look over there.'

Mr Helium saw that the professor was following them to their new height and he frowned.

'What's he up to?' he said angrily.

'Try going down now,' said Max.

They pulled the vent and the balloon sank sharply, only to be followed by Professor Sardine's balloon, which was getting rather close.

'He's after us!' said Mr Helium. 'What on earth can he be planning this time?'

'Let's go up again,' said Max.

So they turned on the burner and up they went, again to be followed by the wicked professor. Then, when they had gone up and down at least six times, Maddy gave a shout.

'Look out!' she said, snatching the vent rope and letting out some air.

She acted just in time. From the profes-

sor's balloon, curving through the air, there came a deadly arrow, aimed right at their balloon. It was only Maddy's swift action which saved the day. Had they not suddenly sunk when she pulled the vent, the arrow would have pierced their balloon and burst it. It would have been dreadful.

They sank for a while and then, on Mr

Helium's instructions, the burner was fired and they shot up again. At this point, Professor Sardine fired up his own burner to come after them. But nothing happened. His gas cylinder was now empty and he had to connect the pipe to the spare. Max and Maddy watched as he fumbled with the hoses. Then, when all was connected, Professor Sardine turned on the tap.

And that was when the funny thing happened. In fact, it was so funny that Max, Maddy and Mr Helium all nearly fell out of the basket with laughter. The cylinder to which he had attached the burner was not a gas cylinder at all – it was a fire extinguisher! And as the tap was turned on, clouds of white foam spurted out of the burner and covered the professor from head to toe. What is more, this made the tap too slippery to turn off, and the foam continued to spew forth.

With no new hot air, and getting heavier every moment with the gushing foam, the professor's balloon sank slowly towards the ground. Mr Helium guided his balloon down behind it, keeping just close enough to witness the hilarious event. So they had a good view of what happened when the professor's balloon struck a tree on the way down, burst with a big pop, and tumbled its wicked occupant into . . . a pigsty!

The pigs were furious. They rushed out of their sheds and nipped the foam-covered balloonist, driving him out into the mud. There were squeaks and grunts aplenty, and not all of them from the pigs.

Up in the balloon, when Mr Helium had wiped the tears of laughter from his eyes, he turned to Max and Maddy.

'What a wonderful, wonderful trick!' he said. 'I wonder who changed the cylinders round?'

Maddy looked at Max. She knew her brother, and she had a pretty good idea that this had been one of his famous plans.

'Max?' said Mr Helium. 'Was it you?'

Max smiled. 'Well, at least it worked!' he said modestly.

They resumed their trip and found good winds. In fact, the winds were so good that they were able to cross into Canada and reach Vancouver that very afternoon, just in time to see the winning balloon sail over the finish line. It was Bonzer Williams, with the Montgolfier twins a close second and themselves a comfortable third.

'Beaut!' Bonzer Williams cried. 'Fair double dinkum!' This is the Australian way of saying that everything had worked out very well and that he was very happy. And so would you have been, I suspect, if you had just won a golden balloon worth one million and one dollars, and raised lots of money for the Home for Children Whose Parents Have Disappeared in Balloons.

There was a great crowd to meet them. The people of the city were all very excited and had turned out in their hundreds, bringing with them thousands of party balloons which they released to welcome the fearless balloonists. So the sky was filled with balloons of every colour and shape, big ones and small.

The president of the United States sent a message of congratulations and the first lady was kind enough to send another cake for Max and Maddy. This was an even bigger one, with a balloon drawn in icing on the top. They sat and ate it at a celebration picnic with the other balloonists, including Honoria and Dolores and Mr Zambuck, who had all travelled to Vancouver (by plane) especially to share in the fun.

Everyone was very pleased with the cake, which was just the right size and extremely delicious. Some cakes are too soggy and heavy. But this one was so light it almost floated. In fact, when you lifted it up, it actually *did* float. It was filled, thought Max, with little bubbles of helium. How remarkable!

And that was the end of the bursting

balloons mystery. Mr Helium was happy, as were all the other balloonists. Max and Maddy were delighted that they had been able to help, and as for Professor Claude Sardine, well, as you can imagine, he was quite furious. Landing in a pigsty and getting covered with mud might well have taught him a lesson, but I'm sorry to say it did not. He remained as bad as ever, and even while wallowing in the pigsty he was plotting his revenge.

But don't worry too much about that. As we have seen, he is no match for Max and Maddy, the famous detectives. They have outwitted him twice now, and I'm sure that they will manage to do so again!